Foul Shot

a novel

by

PAUL KROPP

H·I·P Books

HIP Sr.

LIBRARY AND ARCHIVES CANADA CATALOGUING IN PUBLICATION

Kropp, Paul, 1948–
    Foul shot / Paul Kropp.

(HIP sr)
ISBN 978-1-897039-25-0

I. Title. II. Series.

PS8571.R772F69 2007   jC813'.54   C2007-901268-X

General editor: Paul Kropp
Text design: Laura Brady
Illustrations drawn by: Catherine Doherty
Cover design: Robert Corrigan

2 3 4 5 6 7   14 13 12 11

Printed and bound in Canada

High Interest Publishing acknowledges the financial support of the Government of Canada through the Book Publishing Industry Development Program (BPIDP) for our publishing activities.

The Cougars haven't won a game in years, but Luther sees a way to break the losing streak. There's a big kid named Frank who's just come to their school. He can run plays and sink baskets. Soon Frank turns the Cougars into a dream team . . . but only for a month.

CHAPTER 1

The Ref Is Blind

The score was 52-13.

52 for them.

13 for us.

"We stink," Luther said. He was sitting beside me on the bench, out of breath.

"Nah. It's the lousy refs," I told him.

He looked at me, not much, but just enough.

I turned and looked out at the game. The other team's big center grabbed a rebound. In no time, he put it back in to make the score 54-13. I shook my head and looked down at my Jordans.

"Yeah, we stink," I sighed.

"And we don't have no height, DeShawn, except maybe you."

I'm six-two. That's a decent size for most things, but not in basketball. By the time you reach senior ball, a lot of guys are six-five, six-six. There are even a couple of guys getting close to seven feet tall. Those big guys aren't fast, and not all of them can shoot, but they're way up there.

Our team was pretty small. For some reason, the Cougars seemed to get all the little guys. Our best forward only comes up to my shoulders. He's a great shooter and has some quick moves and all that – but he's short.

Today, up against Amherst, we all felt like midgets. The Amherst center was six-six, and he was *good*. I put the italics in to show just how good he was. And those guys knew what they were doing. I think they must have had two dozen plays in their playbook. Any time we figured one out, they'd shift to something else.

So we were losing, bad. Now it was 56-13.

"DeShawn, Luther, back in," the coach barked.

Two other guys came off, and we were on the court. Luther and I are first-string, about as good as we've got. But those Amherst guys could dribble and shoot around us like we were half dead.

"P&R," Luther shouted. That was our code name for pick-and-roll, a pretty basic tactic. It was still our best move. At least, it worked pretty well in practice.

Luther and I took the ball down, nice and easy. When we got into the front court, we were ready. Luther passed hard to me. I faked to the right and checked the screen at the same time. Then I bounce passed back to Luther, but an Amherst guy was right there. So much for P&R.

The Amherst guy, Henkel, was short and quick and nasty. He started hassling Luther right away.

Luther faked one way, then stepped back and went up. Henkel went up right against him, bumped him off balance, and then blocked Luther's shot. Another Amherst guy grabbed the ball.

The crowd roared.

Nasty but fair, I said to myself. We messed up the play and lost the ball, simple as that.

But what happened next wasn't fair. When Luther came down, Henkel kneed him – right *there*. It was no accident. Henkel just did it, grinning as his knee connected.

Luther fell to the floor. A ref blew his whistle. I was over there in no time, helping my buddy to his feet.

"Charging," the ref called. "Ball to blue!"

There was a smile on Henkel's face. He'd fooled the ref.

"Charging?" I cried.

"Charging?" Luther screamed. Luther had just gotten his breath back and now he was yelling. "The guy was all over me."

The ref turned his back and started walking away. "Player control foul. Ball to blue," he said again.

But Luther wouldn't let it go. He ran over in front of the ref and got in his face. "That guy knees me, right here, and you call a foul on me!" Luther screamed. "On me? Are you blind? Are you stupid?"

I tried to pull Luther away, but he's strong when he gets mad.

"What's with you, man?" Luther shouted at the ref. "These guys *pay* you to be blind? These guys *pay* you to look the other way?"

The ref looked at Luther, then pointed at the bench. "That's a T and you're gone!" he yelled back in Luther's face.

Luther was so mad, I thought he might take a swing at the ref. But Coach G was already there, and he pulled Luther away. The ref blew his whistle again, and Amherst got two free throws for the technical foul. Henkel, the Amherst guy, made both of them.

58-13, and it wasn't fair. Luther should be shooting the foul shot. The Amherst guy should be sitting on the bench.

But now Luther was benched, and the Amherst fans were going wild. Three minutes left in the game, but it was hopeless. We lost 66-15.

After the final buzzer went, I sat on the bench with Luther. He was still steaming mad.

"I can't believe that ref," he said.

"Me neither," I told him. "The guy had it in for us, from the start."

"No wonder we lost," Luther said.

"Yeah, no wonder."

Of course, that wasn't the whole story. The ref was just one problem. The real problem was our team. Our guys – the Cougars – just didn't win games. We had something like a 0-50 record over the last couple of years. So maybe that's why nobody came out for basketball. We had a decent first–string and maybe half a second–string. That was it. Some games, we didn't have enough guys even to sub in.

And we didn't practice – or at least, we didn't practice enough. Our guys had maybe five good plays down pat. But we kept messing up the little stuff. We'd guard a guy for more than five seconds. We'd even mess up a fast break. The plays would go okay in practice, but then fall apart in a game.

"You know our real problem," Luther said.

"What's that?"

"Height," he said. "We don't got no height."

"We don't have *any* height," I told him.

"You and your church talk," Luther snapped back. He wasn't really mad. He picks on me because I go to church on Sundays. I pick on him because his grammar stinks. We're still buddies.

"If we had height, DeShawn, we might be able to get some boards. We might be able to score some points. But right now, we just got . . ."

"Me."

"Yeah, you," Luther said. "And you're good, but not that good."

"You too," I shot back.

"So I know what we've got to do," Luther said. "We've got to find a guy – a big guy – and get him to play."

"You got somebody in mind?" I asked him.

Luther smiled at me. "I think I saw him," he said. "Up in our stands. A great big guy . . . must be new to the school. I mean, anybody that big has got to know how to play ball. You know what I mean?"

I sighed. "Sure, Luther. Anything you say."

"I'm not kidding, DeShawn. This could turn it all around. You start taking notes on all this. Maybe you can turn it into one of them stories you like to write."

"One of *those* stories," I said, fixing it up.

"Sure, DeShawn. Anything you say."

CHAPTER 2

The New Guy

We were standing out in front of the school. There was snow coming down, but it was dry snow so no good for snowballs. In weather like this, most of the kids went inside. But we'd been waiting for a good half hour. Luther kept swearing he saw a big guy way up in the stands. He was certain the guy went to our school, that he had to be some new kid. So we huddled against the cold and kept our eyes open.

"This is stupid," I said. I was freezing and just wanted to get inside.

"Not stupid," Luther said. "Just desperate. The Cougars are desperate, man."

We must have been very desperate to do this, I thought. Waiting around for some kid that maybe went to our school. And maybe he was tall. And maybe he could play ball. Too many *maybes* for a cold day in December.

"Look over there," Luther said. "You see him?"

And I did. Coming down the street was a guy wearing a hoodie and junky old winter coat. He looked like most of the other kids at school, but this guy was big. I mean, he was *big*!

"So what are you going to say?" I asked Luther.

"Not me, man," Luther replied. "I'm the man of action. You're the talker."

"Me?"

"Yeah, you," Luther said, moving forward. "Hey, big guy!" Luther shouted. "We gotta talk to you."

The two of us moved in front of the big guy and blocked his way.

"Hey, there," I began. "My friend here saw you

13

in the stands the other day, watching the basketball game. That was you, right?"

The big guy nodded. We could barely see his head under the hood.

"So my friend, that's Luther here, he was thinking. You see, we're on the basketball team and we've got a couple of problems."

I think I saw the kid smile. *Like, yeah, anybody could see our problems.*

"For instance, we could use a big guy like you on the team. It's not really that height is all that important, but . . . well, I guess we could use some. So we were wondering if you ever played ball."

"Soccer," the guy said.

Luther jumped in. "We mean, like, basketball. You're a big guy, and all, so we kind of thought you might have played."

"Yeah, I used to," the guy said. "A little. Then I quit."

"Why'd you quit?" I asked.

"Stuff happens," he said with a shrug.

"Well, let me tell you what's happening here," I told him. "We've got a team that needs you. We need somebody big and somebody quick and somebody smart. We can see that you're big. So we're kind of hoping you're quick and smart."

"Yeah, smart enough."

"So come on down to the practice after school. We'll tell Coach G about you, and then you give it a try. We've got some great guys. They all play with a lot of heart, you know, but we're not doing so well. And . . . well, we really need you."

Boy, what a suck. I was almost begging this kid to play, and I didn't even know if he could hold a ball. The stuff that Luther gets me into!

"Yeah, okay," the guy said. "I've got a little time."

"That's great, man," Luther said, smiling broadly. "By the way, what's your name?"

"Francis."

I did a quick double-take. Wasn't Francis a girl's name? Nah, there are two ways to spell it. Still, it didn't sound like a name for a ball player.

"How about we call you Frank?" Luther said.

"Call me what you want," the guy said with a shrug. "But I've got to get to class."

*   *   *

I knew there was something strange about Francis. I couldn't put my finger on it, but he wasn't like the rest of us. For one thing, he wasn't black. I didn't know what he was under that hoodie, but he wasn't black. And then there was that weird name. What kind of parents would call their kid Francis? Good thing the guy was tall, or the other kids would have picked on him big time.

So we told Coach G about him that day. Coach

G is Italian, so his real name has lots of Os and As in it, and it's too big to spell out. But Coach G kind of fits. Anyhow, Coach liked the idea. He said we could use more guys for the team, tall or short.

Then we told some of the other guys. It turned out that Ollie had already seen the new kid in the halls. He had the same idea we did, but we got to him first.

Our center, a guy named Cyrus, wasn't too wild about a new player. For one thing, he'd be the one to get bounced by a new, tall kid. Still, even Cyrus knew we had to do something. So did the other first-string players. Our two forwards, C.J. and Marcus told us we might just save the season.

I wasn't so sure about that. We were already eight games into the season – eight losing games. The chance of turning it around now was small. But any chance beats no chance. As my dad used to say, if winning isn't everything then why keep score?

So there we were – nine of us, counting Coach G. We waited for maybe ten minutes, but Francis didn't show. The other guys kept shooting looks at

Luther and me, but all we could do was shrug. Maybe the kid had backed out. Maybe he'd heard about how bad we were.

Then the gym door banged open.

"Oh, sorry," Francis said as he came in.

That was the first time I'd ever seen him without a hoodie. He looked different, at least, different from us.

"He's a Chink," Luther whispered.

"Watch it, man," I whispered back.

"I mean, he's Asian," Luther went on. "I didn't think they could grow so big."

"Shows what you know," I shot back. "Heard about Yao Ming from Houston?"

Coach G walked over to say hello. Then he brought Francis over to meet the team. I think all of us were looking at him with our mouths open. It was like we were in awe – or amazed – or something like that.

"Okay, Francis," Coach G said to him, "Luther said you used to play."

"Used to," Francis replied.

"Well, we were doing a little passing drill. You

know – chest pass, bounce pass. Nice and easy. You ever do that kind of thing?"

"Sometimes." Looks like Francis wasn't a big talker.

"Okay, let's get started."

Coach threw us a couple of balls. We got in a circle and started passing the balls around, not too fast at first. Luther passed to Francis, then he passed to me. Bounce pass. Chest pass.

Boom. The ball came at me like a rocket.

"Whoa, easy man," I told Francis.

"Sorry," he said.

We passed to the right, then to the left. That's when Luther got the pass. I thought my friend might fall right off his feet. It looked like the new guy could pass.

Coach G threw out some more balls. "Okay, everybody get a ball. I want to see you dribble around the gym. Start slow, but when the whistle blows, *move.*"

So we dribbled around and around. At least most of us. Cyrus was lousy at dribbling so he kept losing the ball. Ollie liked to show off by changing

19

hands. Then Coach G blew the whistle and yelled for us to move.

All of a sudden, Francis was dribbling around the gym like a crazy guy. I looked up to watch him move, and then I lost my own ball. So did a couple other guys.

"Looks like the new guy can dribble," Luther told me.

"Yeah, but can he shoot?"

The answer came pretty quick. We got all set up to run lay-ups – two lines, one shooting, one rebounding. It's a pretty simple drill. It was real simple with Francis.

He never missed.

He must have done twenty lay-ups and nailed each one. He could have dunked the ball if he wanted to.

When it was over, we were all staring at him.

"Francis," Coach G asked, "can you do that in a game?"

"Never tried," Francis replied. "My jump shot is better."

So Coach put Francis on the foul line and then

started feeding him the ball. One – two – three, all in the basket, four, swish, five, off the rim. When it was over, Francis had sunk eighteen out of twenty. *From the foul line.*

Coach G kept shaking his head. Then he asked Francis to shoot from the three-point line. Same story.

"Ollie, see if you can pressure this guy," Coach said.

So Ollie got between Francis and the basket. He tried jumping up. He tried to get in Francis's face. He tried everything, but there was no stopping Francis.

When the practice was over, Coach brought us all together.

"Boys," he began, "I know we haven't done well the last couple of games. Okay, the last couple of years. But we've got some new talent here. And I have a hunch things might just turn around for us."

"Yeah!" we all screamed.

"Luther and DeShawn," Coach said, "at lunch, you start teaching Francis some of the plays. We'll do a full practice on Thursday. And then we've got a game on Friday. So what are we gonna do on Friday?"

"Win," we shouted.

"Come on," Coach G yelled. "Say it like you mean it. What are we gonna do?"

"WIN!"

For the first time in ages, maybe we would.

CHAPTER 3

The One-Man Show

The game on Friday was against Gormley, a school on the other side of town. They were an okay team – nothing great like Amherst – but okay. They had height and speed, but their shooting was weak. Lots of shots, not too many points.

They had still killed us last time. We couldn't get the rebounds, so they just kept on shooting. Just as Luther said, we needed height and speed.

Now, at least, we had some height.

"What do you think, man?" I asked Luther. We were in the change room, getting ready.

"That is one weird guy," Luther replied. "I mean, he's a good player and all, but he never talks. He never even smiles."

"Might be nice if you'd stop talking so much," I said. What's an insult or two between friends?

"Might be nice if you could shoot the ball, DeShawn."

"Might be nice if you could even pass, fumble fingers."

Then we both laughed. Luther and me have been friends since we were in grade two. I mean, we learned how to *read* together. At least, I learned how to read. Luther learned how to fake it.

"You see his running shoes?" Luther asked. "I mean, they're really beat up. It's like they came back from some war zone."

"So, is this a fashion show or what?" I snapped back.

"Yeah, I guess," Luther said. Then he shrugged and put on his outfit. "Still, it doesn't make sense."

I just shook my head. I kept hoping that Luther would focus on the game. The coach had made Francis a forward. That kept Cyrus happy. He liked to take the opening tap. It also gave us a guy like Ollie who could really shoot under the net.

We had just one real play – feed it to Frank. That was his name now, at least his basketball name. As a team, we had only one job on offence – get the ball to Frank. The rest of us, we could try to do a weave, or pick-and-roll, or the scissors cut. But we never got those right, anyhow. So now we had one play.

Feed it to Frank.

There was a buzz in the stands when we came out on the court. Frank was number 42, maybe because it was our biggest jersey. There was a lot of noise when he came out. I think the word was going around. The Cougars had a new guy, and the new guy was good.

We got out on the court and got ready for the tip-off. I looked at the guard next to Frank. The guy didn't even come up to his chin.

The buzzer blew, and the Gormley center

knocked it to his guys.

Suddenly, we were on defence. The big-D. We had been so busy with offence, the big-O, that we didn't work on this part of the game.

And it showed. The Gormley guys took it down, then did a simple give-and-go to get it right past us. Up and in: two points. It didn't matter if we had the biggest guy out there. The Gormley team were faster and smarter.

Luther and I took the ball down the court. Then Cyrus joined us and we had a 3-on-2 fast break. The ball could have gone to either Luther or Cyrus, depending on who was free. But we all knew where the ball was going.

Feed it to Frank.

Cyrus bounce passed to me. I looked inside to Cyrus but kicked it over to Frank. Frank lifted the ball, did a lazy jump shot . . . and it was in. Simple as that.

Then we were back on D. The Gormley guys brought it down, but I was able to grab at the ball and knock it to Luther. Then Luther pushed it up the floor to Frank. And then the big guy started to move.

He dribbled down the court faster than I can run,
then did a perfect lay-up into the basket. Nah, it was
closer to a dunk. Frank is so tall that his lay-ups are
almost a dunk. Number 42 is one *biiiig* player.

So we played a really good game. Okay, maybe
our defence wasn't that good, but so long as you
score a lot of points, who cares? The Gormley team
didn't find a way to stop Frank until the second
half. Then they switched to man-to-man defence.
Or maybe it should be two-man-to-Frank defence.
They still couldn't stop his jump shot. And that left

Ollie open to take shots from his side.

58-36 was the final score.

That deserves writing it out. *Fifty-eight for us; thirty-six for them.* It was the first win for the Central Cougars in more than fifty games.

The people in the stands were screaming. I thought they might come storming down to lift Frank up on their shoulders. It really was a one-man show. Frank scored 42 of our points. Ollie got most of the rest, and even Luther picked up a couple.

We were feeling pretty amazing in the locker room. A win! A victory! No one on the team could remember our last victory.

Coach G tried to keep us from going nuts. "Now listen up," he began. "You had a win today, and you should be proud of it."

"Proud is my middle name!" Luther shouted out.

Coach gave him a look. "But we've still got a lot of games to play. We only had one play today, and it worked. But next time, they're going to figure it out sooner. We need to do more than feed the ball to

Frank, you hear me?"

"We hear you, Coach!"

"We're going to practice. We're going to get smarter. And then we're going to win some more – that's the plan. So what are we gonna do?"

"Win!" we shouted.

"I didn't hear you."

"WIN!" we screamed.

"Just like today," Coach finished up.

After we got changed, a bunch of us decided to go out for pizza. I guess it was Luther's idea, but we were all in on it.

"You coming with us, Frank?" Luther asked. "I mean, number 42 ruled the court. You were the hero of the game."

"Can't," Frank replied.

Luther just stared at him. This was our first victory in, like, forever. And Frank was just going home?

"Can't why?" Luther asked.

Frank put on his hoodie and pulled on his boots. "Just can't. I've got things to do." And then Frank was out the door.

"Can you beat that?" Luther said to me. "That Chink is weird."

"Maybe not so weird," I told him. "Maybe he doesn't want to hang out with somebody who keeps calling him a Chink."

CHAPTER 4

The Mystery Man

The Cougars were looking pretty good by Christmas. With Frank on the team, we won all five December games. Our team now had its best record ever. We kept getting more and more fans at the games. Once, even the cheerleaders came out to cheer for us.

I guess it went to our heads. Luther kept on bragging. Ollie did a wonky rap on "We Are the Champions." Even C.J. began to walk around like he was king-something-or-other. I guess we all felt we couldn't lose.

Then we had a Christmas lay-off. Two weeks with no games. Coach G had the gym open for practice, but none of the guys bothered to come. We had Frank, so who needed practice?

One day, I met Luther at the mall. I had to do some shopping for presents. And Luther just wanted to hang out. He says he doesn't have money for presents. Still, he's got lots of cash for fancy coffees.

"So how about that guy Frank, eh?" Luther asked me. He was sipping this coffee that left white foam on his upper lip.

"He's good," I said. "Real good, but not great. He's lousy on D, for one thing. And he loses it when the other guys get in his face."

"Yeah, but look at his shooting and his speed, man. And he's just in grade 10. Think how good he'll be next year. Our team will be – what's the word – incorrigible."

"Wrong word, Luther," I told him. "We'll be unbeatable."

"Whatever," Luther said with a shrug. "And just remember who found the guy."

"That would be you, Luther."

"So who really saved the team?"

"That would be Frank, you jerk. Don't let all this go to your head."

"What's wrong with my head, DeShawn?"

"For one thing, it's ugly. For another thing, it's getting fat. For a third thing . . . well, I can't think of a third thing. But I know there is one."

Luther grinned at me. We'd been doing these jokes for a long, long time.

We just finished our coffee when Luther saw Frank walking down the mall. It was hard to miss a guy that tall. But Frank wasn't dressed like a guy who was shopping. He didn't have on a coat, and he didn't have any bags with presents.

Instead, he had on a pair of overalls. And he was pushing a pail with a mop.

"Looks like our number 42 has a job," I said to Luther.

"How about that?"

"He's trying to make a little money over Christmas. That makes him way smarter than you, Luther. You just like to *spend* money."

"Shut up, DeShawn. Just 'cuz you're rich and I'm not, that don't mean a thing."

Luther had a good point. My family did have more money than his. But not that much more. And we'd been friends so long, what difference did it make?

"Okay, okay. So do we go up and give Frank a high-five?" I asked.

Luther thought about it for a second, then shook his head. "Nah, better not. He's got a job, is all. No sense bugging him. It's no big deal."

"Yeah, no big deal," I said. "Except that we don't know a thing about this guy. He shows up for basketball, plays great, then leaves. He's a mystery man."

"And he likes it that way," Luther said. "You got to respect that."

"I'm not dis-respecting it. I'm just saying."

"And I'm just saying . . ."

By this time, Frank was gone. Our mystery man had a job. That's all we knew. Where did he come from? Where did he live? How did he get to be so good? Those were all good questions. Trouble was, we didn't have answers.

CHAPTER 5

Trash Talk

It was our third game in the new year. We were up against Amherst, the best in the league. Last time, they killed us. This time, we had Frank.

Luther and I were joking around before the game, like always.

"You know what's funny?" Luther asked me.

"Your face," I said.

"No, really," he went on, not missing a beat. "It's funny that our team is, like, all black guys. Okay, maybe Marcus is white, but the rest of us are all black. You know what I mean?"

"Yeah, so?"

"But the best player we've got is a Chink. Can you beat that?"

"He's Asian," I told him. "Can't you get it? They don't like the word Chink. Besides, he might not be Chinese. Maybe he's Japanese. Maybe he's Philipino. Who knows?"

"Yeah, yeah, I got it," Luther said. "But anyway, isn't it funny that our best guy is Asian? Doesn't that beat all?"

"It's ironic," I said.

Luther shook his head and gave me this look. "DeShawn, you gotta stop using those big words with me. It's gonna mess up my head."

The news about our team had spread pretty far. Kids from our school came just to see the big guy play. Guys from other schools sent scouts to see our team in action. No one could believe this amazing guy.

Of course, the rest of us were playing better, too. You get a kind of confidence after a while. And

39

you play better when you know the team has a chance of winning. So Ollie was making those hook shots. C.J. was setting picks so Marcus could come in and get an easy lay-up. And even Cyrus was sinking some jump shots, just like Frank.

Last time, we didn't have a chance against Amherst. This time, it was the other way around. The word was out – we were going to cream them.

So we began doing our pre-game warm-up. We passed the ball around, then ran in lay-ups on our basket. Most of the guys were looking good. Ollie didn't miss even one of his lay-ups. Our only problem was the big guy. Frank kept missing his jump shots. He'd hit the rim or bounce too hard off the backboard.

"Just bad luck," Luther said.

"Could be he's a little off, today," I said. "Maybe working too hard at the mall."

Luther laughed. "It's just warm-up."

"Yeah," I said. "Then it's our chance to get even."

The starting five went out. The Amherst guard

was over six feet, but still no match for Frank. Even our center, Cyrus, looked pretty tall. I think maybe he'd grown in the last couple months. Now he was even with the Amherst center. Our only problem was Henkel. He was still there, still fast and nasty.

The whistle blew. Cyrus tapped the ball to Luther. Luther brought it down, then bounced it to me. I kept waiting for the guys to do something – weave, or pick, or something. But they just stood there. So I faked one way, and then bounced the ball to Frank.

But my pass was a little off. Frank reached for it, but an Amherst guard was too fast. He stepped into the passing lane and picked it off. In a second, Amherst had the ball. In two seconds, they were coming down at us. In five seconds, Amherst scored the first basket.

"Not looking good," Luther said to me. He was out of breath already.

"I messed up the pass."

"No sense crying . . ." he threw the ball out to me "over spilt Coke."

Spilt milk, is what I thought, but there was no

41

time to say it. The Amherst team was in a man-to-man defence. They had a guy on me right away.

Stupid, I thought. *They'll get worn out in no time.*

But the guy kept hassling me. I handed the ball off to Luther, and then his guy was all over him. And then I saw their plan. Not man to man, but man *hassling* man.

They had two guys on Frank. They were double-teaming our big guy. Even worse, one of those guys was Henkel. I could see him in Frank's face. I couldn't hear what he said, but I knew it was trash talk.

Frank kept trying to get clear. There was a lot of pushing, but the ball was still back with us. At last, Frank got kind of clear, so I passed to him.

In no time, Henkel was jumping right in Frank's face. He was still shouting, still trash talking. Frank dribbled and set up for a shot, but Henkel stayed right with him. Frank went up for his shot, and Henkel jumped. He wasn't tall enough to block, but he was loud enough to bug Frank. Trash talk. They were throwing trash talk in Frank's face.

So Frank's shot missed. Amherst got the ball and we hustled back on D.

The Amherst offence was good, but we stopped them and got the rebound after they shot. Then we brought it back to their half. The same thing happened. Two guys in front of Frank, trash talking. Henkel was so close he was almost spitting in Frank's face.

Frank tried to run his man off on a screen. He cut hard to the key and back to the ball, but he just couldn't get open.

I could see that Henkel was grabbing Frank's shirt, but the ref didn't see a thing. Another blind ref!

At last we got the ball to our big guy. Then there were two seconds I'll never forget.

Frank dribbled to get to his position. Henkel stayed with him. Frank took the ball in two hands. Henkel said something – something I couldn't hear. But it was enough.

Frank pounded the ball into the guy's chest.

Henkel flew backwards. He made a big show about falling down, and the ref blew his whistle.

Frank stood there. I don't think I've ever seen somebody that mad. He stood there with the ball in his hands. I think, if Henkel had gotten up, Frank would have hit him again.

"Foul on 42. Ball to Amherst," said the ref.

But Frank didn't let go.

"Ball to Amherst," the ref repeated.

Frank just stood there. I could see his brain working. He was ready to deck the Amherst guy, he really was.

I got over there fast.

"Let it go," I told him. I tried to get the ball out of his hands. "It's just a game."

"It's a ___ game!" Frank shouted. Frank took the ball with both hands and threw it at the floor.

The ball bounced into the air, sky-high.

And Frank stomped out of the gym.

CHAPTER 6

You Gotta Play

We got killed. Without Frank, we had no offence. Our D was never all that good. So Amherst just killed us.

But the next day, it all got worse. Frank didn't show up for practice. We kept waiting for him to show, but he never did. It was just the rest of us, running drills, hopeless as ever.

Maybe halfway through the practice, Coach called us over.

"We've got a problem," he said, "a big problem."

"Frank," I guessed.

"Yeah," replied Coach G. "I talked to his mom on the phone after the game. She says he's quitting the team. He wouldn't even talk to me."

"Maybe he's just mad," Luther said. He still had this stupid grin on his face. "I mean, we've *seen* that guy get mad."

"But what if he really does quit?" I asked.

"He can't quit," Luther said.

The two of us looked at him.

"Well, he can't. We need him. I mean, we're nothing without that guy."

"So can you talk to him?" asked Coach G. "You got him out here. Maybe you can bring him back."

"Yeah, no problem," Luther said. But his voice cracked, so I knew he wasn't so sure.

The next day, we got hold of Frank's timetable. He didn't have any classes with us since he was only grade 10. Turned out that Frank had second lunch. That meant that we'd have to skip math to talk to him. We figured it was worth it.

During our lunch, Luther and me worked on the sales pitch. That's what it was. We were selling an idea. The idea was simple: stay on the team. But when you sell something, you've got to offer a bonus to get a deal. And you've got to get rid of the downsides. Get rid of the stuff that might be a problem. I read that someplace. It doesn't matter if you're selling cars or basketball, it's all the same.

So we tried to get ready. What was our bonus? Maybe we could get him out of practice. Maybe he didn't have to play if guys trash talked him. How did we get rid of problems? We'd get Coach G to

talk to the other coaches. Trash talk shouldn't be allowed. Simple as that. We'd get Coach to work on it. And any guy who trash talked Frank, well, he'd have to deal with Luther and me. *After* the game.

"You ready?" I asked as the bell rang.

"Yeah. You?"

"We'll give it our best," I said.

The grade 9 and 10 kids came pouring in. They had lunch after the rest of us, because the cafeteria was kind of small. It was easy to spot Frank. He was like a giant coming in with a bunch of midgets.

He went over to one side of the cafeteria, by himself. I guess he didn't fit in with the rest of these guys. Then he unpacked his lunch and began to eat a sandwich. In no time, Luther and I were across from him.

"Frank, my man," Luther began.

Frank gave him a look – not a friendly one.

"We just wanted to talk to you," I said. "About the team."

Frank looked at me. "I quit the team. End of talk." Then he took another bite of his sandwich.

"Well, that's what we came to talk about," Luther said. He had this grin on his face. He kind of reminded me of a used car salesman.

"We know there was some trash talk last game," I began. "Those guys aren't supposed to do that. We got Coach G to file a complaint. That guy, Henkel, won't do it again."

Luther shot me a look. I just shrugged. Yeah, I was making that up, but so what?

"And we talked to Coach," Luther went on. "We know you've got a part-time job, so if you need to skip practice, it's okay."

Frank said nothing. He chewed his sandwich.

"You were right to get mad, Frank," I said. "Those guys were dissing you, we know that."

"Dissing my mom," Frank muttered.

"That's what trash talk is," I said. "Just stupid stuff. But we're going to make sure that doesn't happen again."

"I already made sure," Frank replied. "I quit."

"But you can't," Luther whined.

"But I did," Frank said. "I told the coach and so did my mom. Besides, I've got a job now. I don't have time for basketball."

The cafeteria got real quiet. It was one of those moments. All the kids seemed to stop talking at the same time. It was like they were listening in.

"Listen, Frank, I don't want to beg you," Luther went on. "We know there are problems. We know you've got a temper. But the team needs you, Frank. I mean, we're nothing out there without you."

I looked at him. Luther might as well have been on his knees.

"I told you," Frank repeated.

"Frank, please?" I begged. "Just give it one more chance."

Frank shook his head. He didn't say anything. We didn't say anything. We just waited. I think the whole school was waiting.

At last, he spoke to us.

"I told you guys, no. And the answer is still no. I'm not going to play. And I'm not going to put up with that crap."

We just looked at him.

But Frank had more to say. "You think it's fun to go out there, some kind of seven-foot-tall freak? And all you guys shouting, 'Shoot it, Frank. Go for it, Frank.' Well, I'll give you a clue."

We waited.

"My name isn't Frank," he said quietly. "It's Francis. And Francis isn't on the team any more."

"Frank, we need our big guy," Luther whined.

Francis shook his head. "Let me give you some advice. You guys could be a plenty good team without me. You don't need a big guy to sink baskets. But you need some plays. And you need some teamwork. Basketball isn't about one guy sinking balls. It's about a team."

We sat there, quiet.

"And remember the first thing I said," he went on. "My name isn't Frank. It's Francis."

CHAPTER 7

On Our Own

We were all in the change room, just before practice. The mood was pretty lousy. It was glum! That's the word. We were all feeling kind of glum.

"So you talked to him?" C.J. asked. He had a stunned look on his face.

"I already told you," Luther snapped. "I begged him." Then Luther looked over at me. "DeShawn, you tell 'em. I almost went down on my knees."

"Almost," I said to back him up.

"So now we're toast," Marcus sighed.

No one spoke. Marcus had kind of summed the whole thing up. The Cougars were finished. We'd had a good month. We were no longer at the bottom of the standings. And now we were done.

"Francis did say one thing, though," I threw in.

"What's that?" C.J. asked.

"He said we were a good team, or could be a good team. He said we didn't need a big guy to dunk balls. We just needed some plays and some teamwork."

"Yeah, great," Cyrus replied. "And then he quits. He says we need teamwork, and then he quits the team. Nice!"

"But you know," Luther jumped in, "the guy is not totally out to lunch. We only had one play that worked – feed it to Frank. Maybe we need some new plays. Maybe we could feed it to Cyrus."

"Or maybe we set a pick so DeShawn can shoot," Cyrus added.

"Or maybe somebody can teach me how you do that 'weave' thing," C.J. said.

"You know, guys," I said. "It sounds like we're starting to get a plan here."

When we got out in the gym, all the guys were talking. Coach G heard us, and then he joined in. It was pretty simple, really. Either we pulled together as a team, or we rolled over and died.

So we pulled together.

Coach G said he'd make up a playbook for the next practice. All the guys promised to study it, then practice it. We had to get a half dozen plays in place for our next game. Had to! Either that, or toast.

And we had to start sinking some baskets. When we had Francis, he scored over half our points. Now it was up to us. We had to *make* those lay-ups. We had to get clear for some jump shots. And we had to get fast enough to get under the basket for rebounds.

That day, we had our first real *practice*. Before, we just goofed around and took shots. Now we were *working* on the shots. We were running the drills like they counted. And all the guys said they'd keep practicing through the weekend.

Coach G had this smile on his face. He'd seen his team come alive, and I guess he felt kind of proud. He'd come in Saturday and Sunday. He'd help us run the plays so many times they'd be hammered into our heads. And maybe, just maybe, the Cougars could stay alive. Maybe, just maybe, we could win without Number 42.

*   *   *

So did we get good right away? Nah, not a chance. That's like a Disney movie. We sucked. We practiced more, and we still sucked.

Coach G came back with a playbook that had 18 plays in it. No way we could do 18 plays! That's what Luther told him, and we were all with him. So we picked the first six and practiced those. Three of them were good against a man-to-man defence, three of them against a zone.

And then we worked on shooting – trying to get a few shots to work. I mean, none of us had NBA stuff. We were street-ball players. We knew how to use our elbows, not our brains.

So the next week, we got killed. We played Gormley, and they killed us. It was like we were *worse* than before. Sometimes a play would work, but most of the time it messed up. And when it messed up, we were hopeless. It was *baa-aad*.

But something funny was happening to Luther. It was like he'd seen the light. All of a sudden, he was our captain and our coach and our smart guy. He wouldn't let us get down. He wouldn't let us give up.

"C'mon guys," he'd say, "we'll run the Donkey." We gave each of our plays an animal name, to remember them.

Then, when the Donkey messed up, Luther didn't give up. "Pretty good, guys. Pretty good. We'll nail it next time."

But we didn't nail it the next time, or the time after that. The plays that worked in practice, they fell apart on the court. It was like we couldn't handle the pressure.

So then – I can't believe this – Luther had us do this breathing stuff. "Breathe deep. Okay, now out. Breathe deep, now out. Feel your blood go slow!"

It was weird, but Luther said he read it in a book.

That was the other weird thing: Luther reading a book. He started to read books about basketball. He read about plays and coaching and shots. Of course, he couldn't do all that stuff, but he was reading.

So the next game, against Milton, we didn't suck so bad. We lost by ten points. That's not much. The last time we played them, they had killed us. This time, they just beat us. And we started to look better. The Cougars started to look like we knew something. We started to run plays like we had a plan!

"Way to go, guys," Luther told us. "We're getting it. We're getting it!"

The guy who really got all this stuff was Cyrus. Not only did he get bigger, he got smarter. His jumper was working better than half the time. And he could really shoot that ball to C.J. or to me. That ball went zooming through the other team like a knife slicing through butter.

One day, I said to Luther. "You know, we could just feed the ball to Cyrus. He's big, like Frank, and he can shoot."

Luther shook his head. "We tried that one already," he told me. "So maybe we score a few more points, but so what? We might win, but nobody gets better."

"We might win," I said.

"Yeah, but it's not about winning," Luther told me. "It's about teamwork."

That made me shake my head. "Luther," I told him. "You read too much."

We finally did win. It took us two weeks of practice and playing, two weeks of real work, but we did it. Of course, it wasn't much of a win. The Dansville team was bottom of the league, just like us. But we played well, like a real team. It was a big win, too: 56-24. We played some good D even as we rolled up the points.

And we *all* rolled up the points. Cyrus got 18 to top the list, but I was good for 12, Luther got 10, C.J. scored 8, and the other guys got the rest. I tell you, winning feels good. Of course, we won games with Francis, but it wasn't really the team. It was just Francis sinking a lot of baskets. This time, all of us were winners.

The next game, we played Danforth Heights. They were a tougher team, so it was a hard game. C.J. fouled out, so we didn't have our best five at the end. Still, we pulled it off. A two-point squeaker. Big Cyrus sunk the winning basket.

Then it was up against Amherst. Again. There was a lot of trash talk. Again. Now trash talk doesn't bug me, but it got to Cyrus. He didn't play his best. And Luther got a little hot under the collar, so he fouled a lot.

To make a long story short, we lost. The score was 42-32. It wasn't a bad loss, but it was a loss.

So we practiced harder. By the next game, against DeGrassi, we were great. We had our six plays down cold. We had a powerhouse man-to-man D. And we killed them: 56-12. We were so good that I even felt sorry for the DeGrassi guys.

That was our season. The record was 6-12, not bad for a team that hadn't won a game in years.

"See what teamwork can do," Luther bragged.

"Yeah. Along with sweat and luck and Cyrus learning to shoot."

Luther nodded. "And you learning some plays." He took a bite out of his pizza and waited. "Now we just got one problem. The semi-finals."

"We're in?"

"Of course we're in," he said. "That's the good news."

"So what's the problem?"

"Our game is against Amherst."

CHAPTER 8

The Semi-Finals

The semi-finals were big time. There were hundreds of people watching. There might even be NBA scouts out there. The local cable TV carried the game. Even my dad was watching, sitting in front of the TV of course.

Luther and I were in the change room before the game. We were both nervous. Wired. His legs bounce up and down when he gets nervous. Me? I bite my lower lip until it bleeds. So we were in great shape.

"Saw Francis last night," Luther said.

"Get him to change his mind?" I asked.

"Nah, just saw him at the mall and had a coffee. The guy is working twenty hours a week after school. It must be killing him."

"But will he play?" I demanded.

"Nope," Luther said. "We don't need him, anyhow. Francis says he might play next year, but this year he needs the job."

I sighed. The game against Amherst would be hopeless . . . but still.

"Found out something else," Luther said. "Francis isn't a Chink."

I shot him a look.

"Really," Luther said. "His mom is from Korea and his dad was in the army. So he's not Chinese. He's more like Tiger Woods, one of those mixed guys."

"How about that," I said.

"Yeah," Luther said. "Makes you wonder where Korea is, eh?"

Luther doesn't do really well in school. He's reading better now – more like the rest of us – but

he still doesn't study. He's lousy in history, pretty weak in science. And geography? You've got to be kidding!

Besides, he wasn't spending his time on school stuff. Luther was our real coach. He was also our cheerleader. And he was the real brains behind the team. If he ever put his brains to work on school, he might even get some good marks. Who knows?

There were lots of cheers when we came out on the court. I think half the school had come out to the game. Our team was on a roll. We had a good record coming in, and a decent shot at the title. It could be the first banner for our school in years.

But we were all nervous. Even warming up, I could feel it. Some of it was the pressure. Yeah, maybe we could win. Maybe we'd go on to the finals. There were lots of friends and family in the stands, pulling for us. Even Francis was up in the stands, sitting with his mom.

But then there was Amherst. They were the one team we were never able to beat. All season long, even when we had Frank, they whipped us. They were smart, and tall, and had lots of attitude. The trash talk was only part of that. They were out to win, not just to play a game.

Of course, we were out to win, too. But we were scared.

"Hands together," Luther yelled when it was game time. "Breathe in! Breathe out! Okay, we can do this. Let's smoke 'em!"

Coach G held Ollie and me back at the start. He wanted us fresh if the team got into trouble. The problem was, we got into trouble right away.

We lost the tip-off. Then Henkel and a guard

brought the ball down to our end, passed twice and sunk an easy one. Our defence was hopeless. Our guys looked like deer frozen in the headlights of a car.

Then Luther called, "Butterfly," and our guys went down in a weave. The play was always perfect in practice. But this time Henkel was right in Luther's face. Our other guard, Armon, tried to dribble but lost the ball. In no time, their big center picked it up. He came down the court, passed to Henkel, and Henkel went around C.J. to score an easy lay-up.

Four-zip in the first two minutes of play. What a start!

We in-bounded the ball and the guys took it down to set up a play. Luther called for a Donkey and that worked. In fact, that guy Henkel fouled Luther when he went up. That gave us the extra point for Luther's foul shot.

Still, we were down 8-12 at the ten minute mark. Coach G sent in me and Ollie and called for a full-court press. This is tough on a small school court but really wears you out on a full-size court.

Still, we had to do something. The Amherst guys kept breaking our press. Somehow we had to stop them.

Luther suggested we change to a 1-2-2 press. And it worked. The Amherst guards kept getting trapped on the sideline, way in their back court. We had three ten-second calls right away.

Meanwhile, we managed to get some plays going. I was being checked by a slower guy and was able to beat him for two quick hoops. Ollie came in with one and big Cyrus got one. So just before half time, we had almost evened up the score.

We were doing pretty well. The comeback was working just perfectly. And then, we got into trouble.

It was a simple play. We called it the Giraffe because the ball ended up with Cyrus. The set-up was good. Luther and I took the ball down and did our return pass move. Ollie set a back screen for Cyrus and our big guy got in the clear. Quick as I could, Luther passed Cyrus the ball.

But just when Luther went up, Henkel came running over. I knew he couldn't get there in time to block the shot. But that wasn't what Henkel had in mind.

Cyrus went up. Henkel ran up and jumped, knee forward. He got Cyrus you-know-where. The ball missed and our big guy went down.

Of course, the ref didn't see Henkel's foul. The crowd saw it, and they started shouting. But the ref was blind. Even with Cyrus on the floor, the ref was blind.

But that wasn't the real problem. The real problem was that Cyrus didn't get up.

Luther called for a time-out. Soon Coach G was out there along with all the rest of us. Cyrus was still down on the floor, still in pain.

"What hurts?" Coach G asked.

"My ankle," Cyrus groaned. "I think I twisted it when I came down."

"Can you walk?" Luther asked.

Five of us helped Cyrus get up, but our center was in big trouble. He must have done something to his leg on the fall. Now he was walking like a guy who should be in a wheelchair. He ended up on the bench with an ice pack on his ankle.

Cyrus was out of the game. So much for our comeback.

Armon came back on, and we played out the next two minutes. We held Amherst to four points, but we were hurting. Our plays weren't working. Our team wasn't scoring.

The buzzer went for half time. We trudged off the court and into the dressing room. Our team was down six points. Our hopes for the second half were looking grim.

"C'mon guys," Luther told us. "Pull together. We can still do this. We can show those guys."

I just looked at him and shook my head. "Luther," I said. "We're toast."

CHAPTER 9

Sweet!

I sat in the dressing room with my head between my knees. I felt like throwing up. The sweat was pouring off me so bad that it dripped on the floor.

We were killing ourselves out on the court – and Amherst was still killing us. We hadn't had much of a chance at the start. Now, without Cyrus, we didn't have any chance at all.

Then the door to the change room flew open. All of us looked up at the same time.

It was Francis. He stood in the doorway, his head so high it almost touched the top.

"You guys are in trouble," he said. Of course, we didn't need him to tell us that. Anybody watching the game knew that. Anybody even *looking* at us could tell that.

"Yeah, so?" I threw back.

Francis waited a second before he spoke. It was like he had a hard time finding the words. "Maybe I can help. I'll play the last half. That is, if it's okay with you."

I couldn't believe it! I shook my head, just to make sure I wasn't dreaming. It was like some angel had dropped down from heaven. But no, it wasn't an angel. It was Francis standing there. It was Francis, saying that he'd play.

Thanks goodness Coach G kept putting Francis' name on the game sheets. He was still on our team – at least on paper – a month after he'd packed it in.

"Hey, guy, we need you," Luther told him. "We need you back."

"I don't really know your new plays," Francis said.

"Doesn't matter," Luther told him. "The plays aren't working. We're just trying to stay alive out there."

"So maybe I can help you stay alive," Francis declared. "Can somebody loan me a pair of shorts?"

We looked pretty funny coming back out. Francis came out wearing Cyrus's shorts and my T-shirt, and his socks were green. But heck, he was playing for the Cougars. He was Cougars' number 0, but that was better than not having Francis at all.

Our team got a big cheer from the stands when we came out. I bet a lot of the noise was for Francis. The game that seemed so hopeless at half time was looking just a little better. Maybe a whole lot better.

The Amherst team figured it out right away. When we got the tip off, they went to a man-to-man D. They double-teamed Francis again, of course. One of the guards was a big guy. One of them was the trash-talking guy, Henkel.

But that left somebody open on the weak side.

Luther called for a Mule and the ball never even got to Francis, it got to me. I did an easy lay-up to score.

Amherst in-bounded and we went back on D. Then we had some good luck. Their guy Henkel charged into C.J., so the ball turned over to us. Luther and I brought it down. We kept on faking the pass to Francis, but then we ran the Mule again. Another two points! We were only two points down.

Amherst messed up a play on our basket, and then we were on them again. This time, only Henkel ended up guarding Francis. My guard was waiting for me to run the Mule again, so I changed the play. I passed to Francis. It was our old "feed the ball to Francis" play, but it worked.

Francis went up to shoot the tying basket. Henkel went up right in front of him – and whacked his arms. Luther and I both screamed, "Foul!"

This time the ref saw it. A whistle blew. Francis got two free throws.

And – this was the best part – Henkel had made

his fifth foul. Amherst's trash talking star had *fouled out* of the game!

The score was 48-46 for Amherst. But Henkel was gone. We had Francis. We had two foul shots. And we still had twelve minutes to play.

There was screaming up in the stands. Our guys were screaming because we were so close. Their guys were screaming because Henkel was one of their best. The noise seemed to go on and on, until Francis stepped up to the foul line. Then it got quiet.

Francis looked so calm as he set up. One dribble, then two. And then the soft one-hand shot. Swish!

More screaming from the crowd. "Who is that guy?" "Look at that!" "I can't believe it."

Then the second shot: to the backboard, to the rim, around . . . around . . . and in!

Tie game!

Luther was jumping in the air like a crazy guy. "I told you we could do it!" he screamed. "I told you we could get it back!"

"Yeah, but we haven't won it yet," I told him.

"We're going to, DeShawn. The big win is coming. And it's going to be sweet!"

Sweet, maybe. Easy, not a chance.

Amherst put a new guy in to replace Henkel. The new kid was fast and smart. He was also fresh, while the rest of us were getting worn out. Twelve minutes is still a lot of game time.

Amherst was out for blood. They were pushing us hard. The new guy led a five-man weave at us. One of their guys got past Ollie and sunk a quick one. Again, we were down a basket.

Then it was back down to their side. They were using a zone defence now, saving up for the last couple of minutes. We faked the Mule and then fed the ball to Francis. This time he sank it.

That was the game, back and forth, up and down. We got up two points, then lost it; they got up two, then lost it.

The crowd was going nuts. They were screaming for us and for Amherst. They cheered the good plays and booed the ones we goofed up. For the last five minutes, all of them were on their feet. Even Francis' mom was standing up and shouting!

Coach G kept calling time-outs. He knew we were beat. He knew we needed time to settle down and just breathe. He flipped some of us in and out, looking for something that would break open the game.

But the game stayed even. At the last minute, we were tied: 62-62. It was that tight. Both teams were guarding man-to-man, full-court press. With one minute to go, there was no holding back.

Amherst had the ball and they were coming down. My man got past me, but Francis dropped his man and picked up mine. The two of them were face to face, right on the half-court line. And then the whistle blew.

"Over and back," shouted the ref.

There was our break. The Amherst guy had gone back and forth over the line, and the ref saw it. Bonus!

The ball came to us for throw-in at center court. We had thirty seconds left. Luther called for a Giraffe. That was code to get the ball to the center – our big guy Francis.

Trouble was, Ollie didn't set the pick right. I

couldn't get clear so I ended up with no way to pass. The Amherst guy was all over me. I kept waiting for a foul but also kept hearing the crowd in the stands. They were counting with the clock.

"Ten!" they shouted. I had to do something, fast.

"Nine!" I dribbled and kept looking around.

"Eight! There was nobody. I could try a shot, but I was a long way from the basket.

"Seven!" Then I saw something from the corner of my eye.

"Six!" It was Luther charging in from the left.

"Five!" This wasn't any play we'd ever practiced. I wasn't sure where he was going or what he was doing.

"Four!" But there was no time. I got the ball under my guard's arm and bounced it to Luther.

"Three!" Luther got the ball, dribbled once, and went up with a hook shot.

"Two!" The ball hit the backboard, bounced to the rim . . .

"One!" . . . and fell through the net just as the buzzer went off!

Luther screamed.

I screamed.

The fans went nuts.

64-62! The Cougars had won our first playoff game in, like, forever. And Luther sank the winning basket.

Nothing could be sweeter than that.

CHAPTER 10

This Year . . . Next Year

Okay, this is how the Disney movie ends. Our team has just won the semi-finals. We go to the finals. Then we go up against the big, bad team from the city. You know – the big, *baaad* team. They've won every year for fifty years. They foul and cheat and trash talk. Their coach chews sheet-metal instead of gum. Their center is seven feet tall.

But in the Disney movie, the underdogs always win. Our little team, the Cougars, make it to the finals. We're scared to death. We get sick. We throw up in the dressing room. The big, bad team laughs at us. But someway, somehow, we win.

That's the movie.

In real life, it didn't go like that. We went to the finals against a team we'd never seen before. They were from some small town, five hours away. And they were good.

We weren't so hot. Francis never did get most of our plays. He didn't have time to practice. We went into the finals with a prayer. We played pretty well. And we lost.

Sorry. I like happy endings, but that's not how it was.

It wasn't all bad, though. Francis's mom came to the finals. She watched him play. She figured out that practice would help a lot. So next year, Francis is not just on our team – he's *part* of our team.

Then Coach G had a good idea. He got these earplugs at the drug store. They look like little rubber fingers that you stick in your ear. Anyway, the next time there's trash talk . . . in go the earplugs. Luther and me think it's great. We've got

to do something to keep Francis's mind on the game.

Now that the season is over, Luther thinks he might read a real book or two. I told him I was writing this up, so he says he'll read it. In the meantime, he's reading *Captain Underpants*. Because he missed it first time around.

I think my book's better than that. But you be the judge.

ALSO AVAILABLE

Tag Team
by PAUL KROPP

Jes had plenty of problems to start with. He was short, shy and lonely – at least until he went out for the school's wrestling team. Then his life seemed to turn around – until the night he had to deal with Banjo and Joey down in the tunnel.

Running for Dave
by LORI JAMISON

Rusty always felt second-best. He wasn't a winner on the track team or in the eyes of his parents. But when his best friend gets cancer, Rusty is given a challenge he just has to meet.

Shola's Game
by SHAWN DURKIN

Shola has just come to Canada. He feels like an outsider. Back in Nigeria, he was a soccer star, but now he has to learn a new sport. Will hockey help him feel at home here?

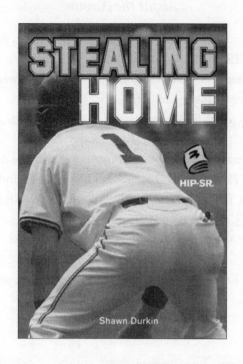

Stealing Home
by SHAWN DURKIN

Josh is trying to fit in with the guys, trying to make his way in a new school. Baseball is the one thing he does really well. But his best friend on the school team is leading him into dangerous territory.

About the Author

Paul Kropp is the author of many popular novels for young people. His work includes six award-winning young-adult novels, many high-interest novels, as well as writing for adults and younger children.

Mr. Kropp's best-known novels for young adults, *Moonkid and Prometheus* and *Moonkid and Liberty*, have been translated into German, Danish, French, Portuguese and two dialects of Spanish. They have won awards both in Canada and abroad. His most recent books are *Running the Bases* (Doubleday) and *The Countess and Me* (Fitzhenry and Whiteside), both young-adult novels, and *What a Story!* (Scholastic), a picture book for young children.

Paul Kropp lives with his wife, Lori Jamison, in an 1889 townhouse in Toronto's Cabbagetown district.

For more information, see the author's website at
www.paulkropp.com

For more information on HIP novels:

High Interest Publishing – Publishers of H·I·P Books
407 Wellesley Street East • Toronto, Ontario M4X 1H5
www.hip-books.com